ADVENTURES
OF THE
ROPE WARRIOR™

A LEGEND IS LAUNCHED

BY DAVID L. FISHER

ILLUSTRATED BY MICHAEL REIDY

GREY PRODUCTIONS
PAPERBACK

The Rope Warrior, Inc.
Chicago

Published by The Rope Warrior, Inc.
600 North McClurg Ct #3109A
Chicago, IL 60611

ISBN 1-889371-01-7

▲WARNING▲

Dedication

To my dear friends, Erin Moore and Jeremy Kraff, for their faith and support. To my family, whose well-meant discouragement only fueled the challenge to prove everyone wrong. And, a special acknowledgement to my editor, Deborah Lewis-Kearns, for her friendship, advice and occasional tug-on-the-reins.

TABLE OF CONTENTS

CHAPTER
The Ropers

1

Approximately 34 million miles from Earth lies an object of varying brightness, reddish in color and completely rusted on its surface. Mars.

By the year 2071, an extraordinary domed space station has been placed there, to house one very special family, the Ropers.

"But what if I don't want to go to Earth?" Charles Roper asked his parents. "What if I want to stay here with you?" He was a little scared as he waited under his bed covers for their answer.

Mike and Betty smiled at each other as they tucked their ten year-old son into bed.

"We understand the thought of moving can be a little frightening," said Mike.

Betty added, "Your training on Earth won't begin until 2078. That's seven years from now."

Charles' parents had given their son the nickname "Skip" Roper when he first started jumping rope at the age of three. Aerobic exercise was an important part of the Ropers' daily routine and jumping rope was Skip's favorite.

The Ropers were the first couple chosen by NASA to live in the domed space station on Mars. Both were in their early forties, but looked much younger. Mike had been a brilliant surgeon and Betty a leading fighter pilot in the Air Force. But to Skip they were just Mom and Dad, and life on the space station was the only one he had ever known.

Betty gently brushed Skip's hair with her fingers, as she tried to calm him. He had straight, dark-brown hair, like his father's.
"Earth is the most beautiful planet in our galaxy," she said. "You'll feel the wind as it blows on your face, and wake each morning to the sound of birds singing."

Mike added, "And you'll meet others your age. Skip, new experiences can be thrilling. Life can be one big adventure."

Mike and Betty each said goodnight and kissed Skip's forehead. As they left the room, they would never know just how exciting (and dangerous) Skip's adventures would be.

CHAPTER

"Code Red... Alien Intruders!"

Skip couldn't sleep. He was thinking of what it would be like on Earth without his parents. This was his day to sleep as late as he wanted, but every time he tried to close his eyes he became even more anxious.

He looked at his alarm clock. It read 4:37 a.m. His parents would be up soon to start their morning exercises.

"I'll just rest here for another half hour and then go jump rope with Mom and Dad," thought Skip.

He began to imagine some new tricks he could try with the jump rope (he knew over one hundred already), and finally began to relax. Gradually, Skip's eyes closed and he fell asleep.

BEEP-BEEP-BEEP-BEEP! Skip tried to keep his head on the pillow as he reached up to hit the snooze button on his alarm clock. He was tired and wanted to go back to sleep.

BEEP-BEEP-BEEP-BEEP! Reluctantly, he sat up in bed and quickly realized that it was not his clock going off, but the "code red" alarm on his forearm communicator.

"OH NO!" he screamed as he pushed hard on the communicator's button.

Mike's frightened face appeared on the small screen. (Skip would never forget that look of terror in his father's eyes.) Mike shouted hurriedly, "CODE RED! ALIEN INTRUDERS! EVACUATE IMMED..." His warning was cut off by the loss of sound and then a static screen.

The Ropers had practiced "code-red" procedures many times, so Skip knew immediately what to do. He leapt out of bed and bolted out the door, sailing through a maze of corridors like a deer running through the woods. Finally, he arrived at the entrance to the space ship. The top of the huge steel door read "EDEN" then below, "NASA, USA."

Skip placed his hand on a small screen to the right of the door. The ship's computer responded, "Access granted," and the door slowly opened. He boarded the ship.

Skip quickly began typing in his 22-digit launch access code exactly in the sequence he learned in training.

The computer's next words snapped him out of a trance-like state:

"Launch authorization approved. Launch time, thirty seconds."

Skip frantically tried to contact his parents with his communicator. "Mom, Dad... Do you read me? Please come in!" There was no answer. He tried again.

"10, 9, 8..." The computer continued the countdown, as the door began closing for launch. Skip decided he couldn't leave his parents behind and ran out of the ship. The heavy metal door just missed him as it closed. He raced through the corridors and had almost made it back when he heard the EDEN launch. Suddenly, there was a loud explosion and the entire space station began to shake! Then everything went black.

CHAPTER
Varco and the Aliens' Attack

Skip opened his eyes, slowly sat up and tried to stand. Everything began to spin around, so he was forced to plop down again. He winced in pain as he felt the large bump on his head.

"Must have hit my head when I fell." He struggled again to stand and eventually made his way back to the main living quarters he shared with his parents.

"Mom? Dad?" Skip called out. But there was no answer. Then he remembered that his father had sent the "code red" signal from the observatory.

"Boy, I hope they're in there."

But when he opened the door, Skip found the observatory empty. All that remained was a towel, a couple of water bottles, and two jump ropes on the floor.

Skip recalled that within the main computer system there was a tracking device for each communicator.

"Computer on," said Skip. "Communicator search," he added. A grid of the entire space station appeared on the screen. There was a green light showing his location in the observatory, but no sign of any other communicators.

Skip was really scared now, but did his best to continue to follow procedures. "Computer... Status report," he called out.

The computer was slow to respond, but finally answered. "Status report. Main computer system - minor damage. Estimated time for self repair - 64 minutes. Communications system - receiver - no damage - transmitter - major damage - completely inoperable. Rehydration system - no damage - EDEN systems - destroyed. All other main station systems fully operational. End of report."

In the corner of the room was the video pod, a floating camera designed to record all space station movement.

The side of the pod was crushed, but it was still running. Did the camera record what happened to his parents?

Skip took out the video tape and walked over to the viewing screen. It took some time for the tape to rewind. To Skip it seemed like a lifetime.

He stared blankly at the video's play-back of the morning's activities. Seeing things from the camera's point of view was hard for Skip. He felt like he was in the room, but powerless to affect the outcome.

The tape showed his parents in the midst of their morning exercises. The two were jumping rope when Betty stopped to take a drink from a water bottle. The camera was focused on Mike, who continued to jump rope. Startled, Mike stopped jumping and pushed the red button on his communicator.

"CODE RED! ALIEN INTRUDERS! Evacuate immediately!" he yelled into the communicator.

But they were upon him just as Mike finished his warning. The aliens were large lizard-like creatures, wearing uniforms and carrying firearms of some kind. The uniforms resembled armor but were made of a more flexible material. It seemed they were prepared to fight.

At the top of the screen, Skip could make out an alien ship. It moved slowly in a hovering pattern over the space station, casting a shadow. Just then, there was a large rumbling. Sensing movement outside the dome, the video pod scanned upwards to see EDEN launching. It was barely off the ground when the alien ship fired a laser beam, destroying EDEN in a blinding explosion of white light.

The force from the explosion rocked the space station. Mike, seeing the Eden destroyed, broke free of his bonds.

"You've killed our son!" he cried as he lunged at one of the aliens and wrestled him to the ground. Though outmatched in size, Mike seized the upper hand in the fight and began beating the creature with his fists.

The others gathered around as if the fight was some kind of entertainment for them all. They snorted, grunted, shrieked and appeared to be cheering on the brawlers.

In the background, the alien ship projected a beam of light into the observatory. A second later, another creature materialized within the beam.

"So that's how they got inside - they transported themselves!" exclaimed Skip.

The Mars space station was equipped with the most advanced Earth technology, but was only capable of transporting inanimate objects. Skip remembered his father's warnings about staying clear of the transport beams. No one noticed the creature as he walked slowly towards the wrestling match.

The first to see him called out his name, "Varco!" and jumped to attention. As each of the others became aware of his presence, they too stopped cheering and immediately scrambled to stand at attention.

Mike continued to struggle with his adversary, oblivious to the others. Standing behind Mike, Varco calmly pulled out a firearm and shot him in the back, immediately paralyzing him. Betty was being held back by another alien, but before she could scream, she too was stunned with

Varco's firearm.

Skip looked on helplessly as Varco had the aliens place two strange devices over his parents' chests.

Each unit, about the size of a catcher's mitt, was connected to a clear plastic bag by a small tube. The devices were activated and emitted a strange glow. Mike and Betty convulsed violently as the glow brightened.

Varco gestured the aliens to deactivate and detach the devices. He held up the two bags, which were empty. Angry, he threw down the bags, pointed his gun at Mike and Betty again and vaporized them.

Varco then called out to the other aliens, "Ichno Bleza Voskwa!" and they began to reboard their ship. While giving the space station one last look, Varco spotted the floating video pod. He approached it, glared into the lens, made several faces into the camera, and then whacked it with his powerful tail. The video pod sailed across the room, hit the wall, and landed in the corner.

A   bloodcurdling   laugh   echoed

throughout the space station. Afterwards, there was only the empty observatory on the tape until Skip entered nearly twenty minutes later.

Skip rewound and replayed the video tape, desperately trying to find answers. He slowed the tape on Varco's entrance and studied every movement, frame by frame. At Varco's glare into the camera, Skip paused the tape. He hit several buttons on the computer and the picture became enlarged, now showing only a neck-up shot of the alien leader.

Skip was frozen at the monitor, transfixed by Varco's cold, lifeless eyes. For hours he sat in silence, the pounding of his heart within his chest was the only sound he heard.

CHAPTER
Skip Makes A Vow

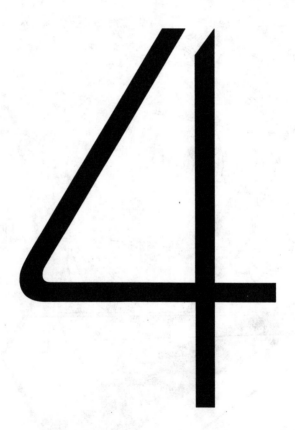

Skip woke the next morning in his bed, not remembering how he got there. "Maybe it was all just a bad dream," he thought, running into his parents' sleeping quarters. Finding it empty, his hopes quickly sank again. He staggered into the observatory.

The towel, water bottles, and jump ropes lay untouched from the previous day's events. Skip picked up the jump ropes and thought back to happier times. He began to cry.

What was he supposed to do now, all alone with no means of contacting NASA. Would someone come for him? Would the aliens be back?

Skip thought about what his parents would have wanted him to do. He missed them so much.

He decided to follow his usual daily routine. He brushed his teeth, bathed, exercised and forced himself to eat...even though he was not hungry. After dinner, he made his first entry into his father's computer diary.

"Our spaceship EDEN has been

destroyed and our communications system is down. Everything else is in working order.

On this, the eleventh day of March in the year 2071, I, Charles Lawrence Roper, though I don't know how long I will be stranded here, vow to use this time to prepare myself both physically and mentally for whatever challenges lie ahead!"

CHAPTER
A Shocking Discovery

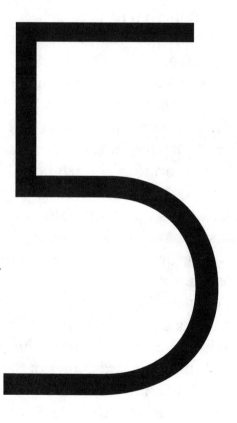

Time passed slowly for Skip. Each day he became more efficient at his daily routine so by the end of the day there was always extra free time. During the first few years alone, he spent that extra time in front of the video monitor grieving for his parents and studying Varco.

He was beyond obsession. He tried to talk with the computer about his feelings, but it wasn't programmed to understand emotions. Each day he spent more and more time at the monitor. Though he still missed his parents, his grief was slowly being replaced by his anger and lust for revenge. This was happening so gradually that Skip had no idea he was on a direct course for self-destruction.

One day, Skip heard a noise. He asked the computer if there was any strange presence aboard the space station. The computer replied that there was not, but Skip could still hear a low humming sound.

Skip searched the observatory, but found nothing there. Finally he looked up to discover the video pod following him. He grabbed the pod and yanked out the video tape.

"Must have self-repaired," thought Skip. "Wonder how long it's been operating?"

Skip went over to the monitor and inserted the tape. "That can't be me!"

He tried to adjust the tracking but the picture didn't change. Skip barely recognized himself! He looked crazed and obsessed! Although he still had a human form, his actions and mannerisms were more similar to those of Varco.

His hand trembled as he reached out to touch his image on the screen. "What has happened to me?" cried Skip. "What have I become?"

After this shock, Skip spent some time thinking about his life and how he was spending his time. He decided he must find a more positive way to focus his mind and expend his energies.

CHAPTER
Learning The Ropes

Skip threw himself into his studies. He read his father's books on the sciences and his mother's on space and aero-technology. The computer tested him on a variety of subjects and challenged him with problems of logic and games like chess which teach strategy.

To fill the extra time, Skip went back to rope jumping (he hadn't touched a jump rope since his parents' deaths). Though he exercised regularly, rope jumping was the one activity that had always relaxed Skip. He found his old jump rope, but noticed it was now too short for him. He had grown over the years but his father's rope was still a bit too long for him. He adjusted it to his size by tying several knots in the rope.

Once he became comfortable with the feeling of his father's heavier rope, the old tricks came right back to him. He began his mornings with warm-up exercises, an aerobic jump rope workout, followed by a cool down period and lengthy stretching session.

Nights were dedicated to developing new rope jumping tricks. He mastered twirls, crosses, step throughs, turns, tosses and wraps. There were tricks with speed and power and those that looked like cowboy lariat moves.

The rope never left Skip's side. He jumped with it in the morning, wore it during the day, worked on tricks with it after dinner, and then slept with it at night. He even used the computer, programming movements involved in various rope jumping tricks into the system. The computer in turn challenged Skip to execute new combinations.

As time passed, the rope became an appendage of Skip. He learned to manipulate one end of the rope to open doors, activate buttons, and retrieve, move or throw objects.

Skip   not only grew bigger and stronger, but his power and endurance also increased dramatically. Soon he was tall enough to take the last, extra knot out of his jump rope. He was now just as tall as his father had been.

"Will Dad's clothes fit me now?" he wondered.

The space station had been fully stocked with clothing for a boy at various stages of growth, but Skip knew it was time to check his father's closet for man-sized clothing. As he approached his parents' quarters, he slung one end of the rope out in front, wrapped it around the latch and opened the door.

Everything appeared as it had 12 years before. He went over to the closet, took out one of his father's brightly colored outfits and tried it on.

Just as he finished zipping it up and admiring the fit, he suddenly felt something crawling on his shoulder and down his arm. There was something alive inside!

Skip began to cautiously unzip the suit while keeping an eye on a moving lump which now had reached the bend of his right elbow. He worked his left shoulder and arm free, but as he began to slide his right arm out, the lump stayed near his elbow.

"Just a little farther," thought Skip. Sweat from his brow dripped into his eyes and began to sting, but he managed to stay focused.

Suddenly, the lump began to glow. Nothing could have possibly prepared Skip for the pain that was to follow.

CHAPTER
The Disappearing Lump

"AAAHHH!" he cried. The lump was burning Skip like a hot coal. He grabbed at it with his left hand and burned his fingers. The right sleeve of the space suit began to melt under the intense heat.

Skip sped through the space station to the laboratory. In a corner, there was a glass chamber that looked like a large telephone booth. Inside, there was a pull chain next to a shower head.

Skip rushed in and closed the door behind him. Placing his right arm directly under the shower head, he pulled on the chain and was immediately covered with soothing chemicals. Another pull on the chain released a shower of cool water which soaked the entire chamber.

Skip pulled off the rest of the suit, afraid to look at his right arm. However, when he did look, there was no sign of anything and the pain was entirely gone. There was no evidence of a burn, bite or claw mark. The only trace was a small round discoloration.

"Almost looks like a birthmark," Skip thought to himself. He would soon find out just how right his observation was.

CHAPTER

Searches, Scans & Silhouettes

8

Skip thought that the creature must have crawled out and was loose somewhere on the space station. He knew that the most efficient way to track any living object was to use the computer's help.

"Computer on," said Skip. "I need a thermo-scan of the space station."

It took just a few moments for the computer to respond. "Thermo-scan completed," said the computer.

Skip went over to the monitor to analyze the results and found that he was the only life form registered.

"It's got to be here somewhere," thought Skip.

He brought the suit to the testing area, held the right arm under the molecular scanner and took a reading. Sure enough, there was a foreign substance on the sleeve.

Skip told the computer to analyze the substance and scan the space station for similar molecular patterns. The computer showed a flashing blue light on its grid.

"AHA! Got you now!" Skip anxiously began isolating the reading. He hoped that if he magnified the section that was flashing, he could actually see a silhouette of the creature.

In his haste, he didn't realize that the creature was already in the same room - closer than he had ever imagined.

CHAPTER
It's What's Inside That Counts

"NO! IT CAN'T BE!" Skip exclaimed. He magnified the flashing blip one last time. "NO!"

Skip felt a horrible sinking feeling in his stomach as he stared at his own silhouette flashing on the screen.

"It's inside of me!" he cried. He looked again at the mark on his arm. "Don't panic, stay calm, the read-out shows my entire body...must be some kind of mistake...must find out for sure..."

Skip took a sample of blood from his right arm and put it into several test tubes. He had the computer run a complete analysis of the blood. While waiting for the results, he looked at himself in the mirror and stared at his reflection. Other than the mark on his arm, he looked exactly the same.

"Computer, are the tests completed yet?" "Estimated time of completion, 45 seconds," responded the computer.

Skip went over to the monitor, sat down and mentally prepared himself for the results.

"Okay, let's have it."

The report on the computer screen gave lots of good information about Skip and his general health. But it also stated that mixed in with his healthy blood cells were foreign particles of about the same size.

"What are these?" Skip asked the computer as he highlighted the particles on the screen.

"The highlighted items match the molecular pattern of that which was found on the suit." replied the computer.

"Are they harmful?" asked Skip, feeling frightened of what the computer's answer might be.

"They are tiny organisms made up of substances not currently found on our charts. They entered your body through the right arm and spread throughout your bloodstream. The current status of these organisms is dormant."

"How do I get rid of them?"

"Initial testing reveals that any attempt to remove or alter the organisms would result in their no longer being dormant. Tests are inconclusive as to whether such an attempt would result in extinction of you or the organisms, or both," said the computer.

The computer's diagnosis was not what Skip wanted to hear, yet he felt there was nothing to do but monitor the situation. He remembered his parents had always stressed that positive thoughts and energies were an essential part of staying healthy.

Skip decided that from this point on, each day would be special. He would never take time for granted again.

CHAPTER

Birthday Surprises

10

September 25, 2086, 4:28 a.m. Skip was sleeping on his back. As always, his jump rope was loosely draped around his shoulders. When the clock changed to 4:29, his eyes opened suddenly. His internal clock always knew when the alarm was about to ring. At 4:30, the alarm sounded. Skip slung one end of his rope at the clock and turned off the alarm.

He got out of bed and headed down the hallway to the kitchen. Without breaking stride, he opened several doors along the way with his rope.

"Computer on...oatmeal, bagels, orange juice...and hot chocolate, " he ordered.

The food materialized on the breakfast table. One of the bagels had a lighted candle in it!

The computer began to sing, "Happy birthday to you; happy birthday to you; happy birthday dear Skip; happy 25th birthday to you!"

Skip was pleasantly surprised. "I completely forgot what day it is. Thank you for remembering," he said to the computer.

The computer replied, "I am programmed to acknowledge the date of birth of human life forms on this space station at 5 year intervals."

"I know, I know," said Skip. "But thanks anyway."

He was enjoying his birthday breakfast when he heard a sudden, loud noise from the observatory. He gazed out of the dome just as a large space ship with unfamiliar markings slowly drifted into view.

Skip grabbed a gun and took shelter behind the closet door, leaving a small opening so that he could see out. He waited there in the shadows - gun in one hand and rope in the other.

A high-pitched sound echoed through the observatory as a beam of light came from the ship. The beam touched down about ten feet from Skip. Peering out of the closet opening, he could barely make out the faint shape of something or someone being transported aboard.   As the silhouette materialized, Skip slowly opened the closet door. He dropped his gun and rope to his side. Both objects slipped out of his hands as he stepped out from the closet. His eyes welled with tears. It was finally over.

CHAPTER
Hellos & Goodbyes

They stared at each other. Skip, over-whelmed with emotion, managed to stammer out, "Don't...don't you recognize me, Uncle Joe?"

Joe Taylor was an Earth astronaut who volunteered to check out the space station. He wanted to pay his last respects to his best friend, Mike Roper, and his family. He didn't expect to find any signs of life, let alone the one person who had ever called him "Uncle".

"Skip!" cried Joe, as they threw their arms around each other.

"I can't believe it...after all these years. When the spaceship exploded and there was no further communication, we assumed everyone was dead. What happened?"

"Intruders raided our station and murdered my parents. The spaceship was destroyed with no one aboard. I kept hoping that NASA might send another ship."

With sadness in his voice, Joe said, "When I left NASA, there was no one else to fight for more funding for the MARS program. So they decided to cut their losses and abandon the project."

Just then Joe's pager went off. He pressed a button and listened to a private message.

"They want me back on the ship," Joe said to Skip. "Take what you need and let's get out of here."

"I'm never coming back, am I?"

"Probably not," Joe answered.

Skip had fantasized about being rescued for fifteen years. Now that it was happening, he realized it wasn't going to be easy to leave.

"I need a couple of minutes, Joe. If that's okay?"

Joe nodded, understanding.

Skip took one last look through each room. He stopped at the bridge long enough to touch the computer console.

"Computer on. Goodbye old friend."

"I am experiencing a rare vacancy in my data sensors," replied the computer.

Skip smiled, "I'll miss you too!" he said.

He gathered up the video tape of Varco, tied the rope around his waist and stood next to Joe.

Skip was scared about being transported for the first time. When he heard the high pitched sound, he clutched Joe's arm and closed his eyes tightly. When he opened them again, he and Joe had arrived in a cylindrical chamber.

"How did you wind up on this alien ship, Joe?" asked Skip.

Joe winced. He understood that Skip was unexposed to different life forms and that this was the reason he had used the word "alien". But what would the others who were listening think?

"Hey, who are you calling an alien?" bellowed a voice over the speaker, "Joe, you are to take him to the decontamination chamber to be quarantined until Dr. Bosk can give you both a full medical examination!"

"Yes Gar, I am aware of our procedures," responded Joe.

"Are you?" questioned Gar. "Then how does this awareness explain the fact that you granted a stranger access to our ship without permission?"

As Joe and Gar's discussion became more confrontational, they switched languages - perhaps speaking Gar's native tongue. It appeared that Joe got in the last word. He then put his arm around Skip's shoulder and guided him out of the chamber.

"What was that all about?" asked Skip.

"Gar is the chief of IDP security."

"IDP?"

Joe explained, "It stands for Intergalactical Drug Police. We are a select group of delegates from across the galaxy, hand-picked by the Council. I was chosen as a representative from Earth...and that's really all I can tell you until I speak with Colonel Lotar."

CHAPTER
The Doctor Is In

12

Joe led Skip through a long corridor until they arrived at the decontamination chamber. Dr. Bosk spoke to them over the speaker.

"Please step onto the moving side-walk."

Joe went first and Skip followed.

"Now, place your hands high above your head and keep them there until you reach the end."

They followed Dr. Bosk's instructions. It was like a human car wash. First they were sprayed with a dry orange powder and then showered with a wet green mist.

The sidewalk continued to move them through a series of colored mists and light rays until they reached a warm breeze which dried them off.

"I'll see you one at a time in the examining room," said Dr. Bosk, "Joe, you first."

As Joe headed through the door of the examining room he glanced back at Skip who looked a little nervous. "Nothing to worry about," he said reassuringly, "Dr. Bosk was the finest physician on Krom. Their medical procedures are far beyond those of Earth. You are in very good (Joe paused) hands."

Skip paced around while he waited to be examined by Dr. Bosk. (He was nervous!) No one, except his parents and the Mars space station computer, had ever examined him.

Finally, the electronic door slid open and Skip went into the examining room. Joe was already gone and there was no sign of Dr. Bosk. Skip sensed that something was wrong. Just then another door slid open and a squid-like creature appeared in the doorway. It had one eye in the middle of its large forehead and slimy tentacles instead of arms or legs. Skip drew his rope and readied himself to strike.

"Just stay still and you won't get hurt," warned Skip.

The creature looked at him, puzzled. "I believe you have that wrong...the line is - just stay still, this won't hurt a bit. And that's my line. I'm the doctor."

"OOPS! I beg your pardon, Dr. Bosk,"

"That's okay. I guess you're just a little (pointing at the rope) jumpy," Dr. Bosk said, laughing at his own joke, "now hop up here." He patted a tentacle on the examination table.

Skip hoped Dr. Bosk was a better doctor than comedian, but he politely smiled and laughed along while getting up on the table.

"Computer on," said Dr. Bosk. "I need a Zicarphtune and the Orileonort."

As the devices were transported by the computer, Dr. Bosk turned to Skip and said, "There are no translations for these yet in your language."

Since Kromian medical procedures seemed so different to Skip, he asked many questions during the examination, all of which Dr. Bosk was happy to answer. He was impressed with Skip's knowledge of Earth medicine.

Skip told Dr. Bosk about the creature that had entered his bloodstream, and the Orileonort (used mostly for blood work) confirmed the findings of the Mars space station's computer.

Just as the examination was over, there was a knock at the door.

Joe returned from his meeting with Colonel Lotar with   good news. "Skip, with Dr. Bosk's approval, you will be granted access to the rest of the ship." Joe addressed Dr. Bosk, "Is he cleared yet doctor? I'd like to show him around the ship as soon as possible."

"Overall, he's as healthy a specimen as I've seen on any planet this side of Ruxa," said Dr. Bosk. "His heart beats as strong as a wa-am-bul. Permission granted. In fact, I think I'll join you!"

Skip thanked Dr. Bosk and the trio set out for a tour of the IDP ship.

"This is our communications room," said Joe, as he stood in front of a thick, clear door.

Skip glanced inside and saw lots of different equipment, some of which seemed quite advanced. Just as he was about to get a closer look, a familiar voice yelled to them from behind.

"Not so fast!" Skip wheeled around and came face to chest with the monstrously powerful IDP security chief, GAR.

Joe was quick to respond.

"Col. Lotar and Dr. Bosk have both granted access," said Joe, "Skip is my responsibility."

Joe gestured for Skip and Dr. Bosk to enter the communications room. Gar followed behind, with a scowl on his furry face.

Dr. Bosk led Skip over to the main terminal. Skip was surprised by the huge capacity of the IDP's computer system.

"The IDP can handle transmissions from four different galaxies at the same time," explained Dr. Bosk.

Skip glanced back to find Joe and Gar engaged in another heated discussion.

"What's behind that?" asked Skip,

pointing to the long black curtain covering the far wall of the communications room.

"Detention chamber," responded Joe, as he and Gar joined the two.

Joe pressed a button and the curtain began to open. Skip's eyes widened as the parting curtain revealed two prisoners behind a secured observatory window. Skip put his hands on the glass and drew his face within an inch of it. He was breathing so hard that the window began to fog.

"They look just like Varco!" Skip said, frantically.

Dr. Bosk began to speak, but Skip was unable to take his eyes off the prisoners.

"They're space chameleons from the planet Keebar," explained Dr. Bosk, "Varco is their leader. Many of them function quite profitably as drug running space pirates. These two were on such a mission when Gar's troopers captured them."

"They were carrying a large shipment of raw materials which they brought from Earth to process on Keebar before sending it across the galaxy," added Joe. "Skip, are you okay?"

Skip finally took his hands off the glass and turned around.

"I want to join the IDP," he said, "I want to stay and help you fight my parents' killers."

Joe broke the silence before there were any objections, "I'll see that you are admitted into the IDP's junior deputy program and you can sit in on tonight's strategy meeting. But first let's get you settled into your sleeping quarters."

When Joe and Skip left the room, Gar turned to Dr. Bosk and vented, "Colonel Lotar will hear of this. The last thing we need here is some hot headed kid vigilante messing up the entire mission!"

CHAPTER
What's for Dinner?

13

Skip's sleeping chamber was adjacent to Joe's in the humanoid section of the ship. Aside from the room being a slightly different shade of white, it was quite similar to his old room on the Mars space station.

Skip sat at the computer in his sleeping chamber which was hooked into the main system. He reviewed diagrams of the IDP ship to reinforce what he had learned on his tour.

"I'm starving!" Skip said to himself as his stomach began to growl.

"Will you be eating in your room or joining the others in the Central Consumption Center?" asked the computer.

He hadn't eaten anything since breakfast was interrupted earlier that morning, but had told Joe that he would join him for dinner.

"Central Consumption Center."

Skip found Joe next door and followed him down several hallways to the middle of the ship.

"Something smells good," said Skip

as they approached the Central Consumption Center.

"There's nothing like the smell of freshly baked cracklies - those are for tomorrow," said Joe.

Skip sat between Joe and Dr. Bosk at a table and looked around at the many different life forms. As he glanced from one IDP member to another, he gave each a friendly smile to say "hello".

A somber looking creature was about to pass in front of Skip when Joe blocked the creature's view of him.

"Never bear your teeth to a Tunkskonian!" warned Joe.

"Not even a smile?" asked Skip.

"Especially a smile, " said Dr. Bosk. "It would be the same as me giving you 'the tentacle'."

Now Skip was really confused.

"I'll explain later," said Joe. "Let's eat."

Dinner was served by passing big bowls of food around the table. There were delicacies from many different galaxies and

Skip sampled each main dish.

He tried smoked wa-am-bul, roast hoo-toose and broiled kuh-kuh-a-duh, which he thought tasted a lot like chicken.

Skip found that sampling the galactic dishes was not satisfying his hunger. Dr. Bosk passed him a large bowl. Inside was something he recognized - oatmeal!

"This is my favorite breakfast food and I'm so hungry!" said Skip as he scooped a big ladle-full.

"Hmm," said Dr. Bosk, "Most humans I know don't care for Spindelobytes in mashed Weegumm. It makes me gag."

Skip looked at what he was about to pour into his bowl. There was something moving under the stuff he thought was oatmeal.

"Those Spindelobytes are tricky," added Dr. Bosk, "gotta chew them quickly before they sting you!"

Skip knew that if he didn't put the ladle right back in the serving bowl, he'd never be able to look at oatmeal again.

He felt a bit queasy.

His senses were on overload. There was so much to process - strange tastes and smells from a variety of foods and life forms, and the oppressive noise coming from all the scattered, foreign-tongued conversations.

He closed his eyes and took slow, deep breaths until his stomach settled back into his abdomen.

CHAPTER

"The Solution's a Solution!"

14

After dinner Skip followed Joe and Dr. Bosk into the conference room. Looking around, Skip noticed some familiar faces from dinner and waved "hello" to everyone (except, of course, the Tunkskovians).

A group of highly decorated life forms entered from the back of the room. Dr. Bosk excused himself and joined the group at the head of a long rectangular table. Colonel Lotar banged her gavel and everyone took their seats.

Colonel Lotar was Ruxanian (from the planet Ruxa). Ruxanians are distinguished by their lion-like facial features and the striped pigmentation of their skin.

Skip immediately sensed a nobility about Colonel Lotar. The room was silent. Colonel Lotar pressed a button and the central computer transported ear inserts for everyone. The ear inserts translate all speech into the wearer's native language. They were only worn at important meetings because Colonel Lotar wanted to encourage the exchange of language and culture.

Once everyone had their inserts in place, she began.

"First I'd like to welcome our newest visitor, a descendant of planet Earth, Charles 'Skip' Roper."

There was polite applause from the IDP members.

Colonel Lotar continued. "Joe has issued Skip an IDP junior deputy's badge. He will receive full accommodation upon completion of his formal training."

Gar rose to his feet.

"Point of order," he said, in an irritated tone of voice. "I want to officially register my objection! I understand that Joe has close ties to this human, but as head of IDP security, I believe issuance of a junior deputy's badge is most premature. Not to mention a complete breach of security!"

Colonel Lotar handled Gar's objection with great calm and dignity, noting it for the record. She then called upon Lieutenant Groon to update everyone on the Keebarian drug ring's activities.

Lieutenant Groon was a great war hero from the RL7 sector, and was now more machine than bones and tissue. Dr. Bosk bragged that he had patched Lieutenant Groon back together almost fifty times.

"We have questioned the two captured Keebarians, but they refuse to tell us anything!" said Lieutenant Groon.

Gar stood and spoke with great animation.

"Just give me fifteen minutes alone with them. I'll get them to talk. I know how to deal with their kind."

Lieutenant Groon responded forcefully, "We'll have none of your barbaric tactics, Gar. Now sit down!"

Usually, Gar did not respond well to forceful direction, but he respected Lieutenant Groon and realized that he had disrupted the flow of the meeting. So he sat down.

Lieutenant Groon continued, "We found gallons of this in the cargo bay of the Keebarians ship." He held up a large clear bag filled with a paste-like substance.

"We know they smuggle it from Earth in great quantities and bring it to Keebar, where they process it into the synthetic drug known as Zacknu."

One of the troopers asked, "What about taking-out their processing plant with some strategic bombing?"

"That's a great idea, but it's not quite that simple," replied Lieutenant Groon. "Computer on. I need the holographic scale model of the main Keebarian drug factory."

The computer projected the hologram on to the top of the table. It showed a large building surrounded by a cavernous trench.

Lieutenant Groon continued, "An air strike is too risky because of the heavy anti-aircraft artillery on the roof. We just wouldn't be able to get close enough."

Another trooper stood and pointed to the wooded area on the far side of the model.

"I'd like to recommend a land assault from the west," he suggested.

Lieutenant Groon had thoroughly

analyzed each strategic approach to disabling the unit. However, he also understood the importance of listening to a variety of opinions before making a decision. He was well aware that solutions often come from those who are not so "close" to the problem. Therefore, he encouraged input from everyone in attendance at the meeting.

"Your recommendation is a good one," he responded to the trooper (who smiled), "We would be able to land here in this wooded area and proceed on foot. But we would have trouble crossing this narrow ledge (pointing) which is protected by these four motion sensor laser turrets. If we could get about four troopers across that ledge, I believe I've got a plan that would work. But we must first find a way of getting past the motion sensors. Dr. Bosk has been working on a solution."

"And the solution," said Dr. Bosk as he stood and held-up a test tube filled with a glowing orange substance, "is a solution! I stand before you holding my life's work.

A liquid which accomplishes the amazing task of...repelling laser fire! I call it Lixablak!"

The group responded to the news with a standing ovation, followed by a great amount of excited chatter.

(Was Skip seeing Dr. Bosk blush?)

Dr. Bosk said humbly, "Thank you. Thank you. Now please be seated. To continue, the original plan was to produce enough Lixablak to cover the exterior of the ship and all of our clothing. However, the main compound in Lixablak, Missonium, is so rare that there is only enough to cover about half a space suit."

"What about covering my shield?" questioned Gar.

"Not for this mission, Gar," replied Lieutenant Groon. "Laser turrets fire from four different directions at once!"

Commander Aclovar, a highly decorated weapons specialist and one of the founding IDP members, stood to speak. "What we need is a flexible, lightweight defense mechanism in the hands of our best scout," she said.

Then she addressed Lieutenant Groon, "I can put my staff to work on it immediately!"

Skip had an idea.

"Dr. Bosk, what exactly does Lixablak do?" he asked.

Gar was appalled that Skip would speak out at the meeting, but he kept his objection to himself, for the moment.

"When Lixablak is applied, it creates an energy field around an object so that it cannot be destroyed or penetrated."

"And you said that you have enough of it to cover about half a space suit?" asked Skip.

Gar was becoming increasingly agitated with Skip's participation in the meeting. Oblivious to the pulsing veins in Gar's forehead, Skip continued, "Then you have more than enough to cover my jump rope!"

The room was silent for a moment until everyone broke out in laughter.

Gar was laughing loudest as he rose to his feet.

"I don't see what's so funny," said Skip.

Gar had heard more than enough. He pounded his fists on the table and yelled, "You are a fool and a lunatic! You're going to defeat the Keebarians with that toy? This is your first day and already you have wasted too much of our time. Now keep your mouth shut!"

Joe saw the look of surprise and pain on Skip's face and attempted to quiet him, but it was no use. Skip had never been spoken to like that before and his natural reaction was to defend himself. After all, he was only trying to help.

"But I..." Skip was only able to say those two words before the enraged Gar barked him down.

"What part of 'keep your mouth shut' did you not understand?" he screamed. "I call for a challenge!"

A hush fell over the meeting. In desperation Joe tried to appeal to the Colonel's sense of fairness.

"Colonel Lotar, I request some time for Skip to prepare for such a challenge."

Gar was quick to offer his rebuttal, "He has already received an IDP Junior Deputy badge. I have the right to challenge him or any other badge holder at any time," said Gar.

"Joe," said Colonel Lotar, "did you not inform Skip of the rules?"

"Yes," said Joe.

Gar sneered and turned to Joe, "I won't hurt him... too badly."

CHAPTER

Showdown: Skip vs Gar

15

Gar called for the computer to replace the hologram on the table with two eight-foot Lanuvian staffs.

He hopped up on the table and threw one of the weapons at Skip who reached up with one hand and caught the staff. Gar began shadow fighting with his weapon as Joe guided Skip to the far end of the table.

"He is the best at this type of fighting," Joe whispered to Skip. "Concentrate on your defense. The longer this goes, the better your chances."

The other IDP members moved to the back of the room. Gar and Skip squared off on top of the table.

"No one has ever made it past me to the other end of the table. If you are the first, I will personally see to it that you become an IDP agent," boasted Gar as he snickered to himself and stepped back into a fighting stance.

Skip stepped back as well, threw down his staff, and untied his rope from his waist. He began turning the rope above his head as Gar approached, smiling.

Skip released one end of the rope and hooked it on the light fixture above Gar's head. He tugged lightly on the other end.

"Ha! Missed me! Not as good with that thing as you thought you were!" taunted Gar as he moved in on the seemingly defenseless Skip.

Holding on to the end of the rope, Skip took a leap and swung to the side, around Gar, and landed on the other end of the table. With a flick of his wrist he unleashed the rope from the fixture and caught the other end with his free hand. He stood casually turning the rope at his side as the IDP members gasped and applauded.

"Very impressive young man," Colonel Lotar said.

"When presented with an obstacle, it is sometimes best to think 'outside the loop'," Skip replied confidently.

"Who said that?" inquired the Colonel.

"Well, as a matter of fact I..."

WHACK! Skip was cut off in mid-sentence, as Gar hit him with his staff from behind, knocking him off the table. Gar posed triumphantly with his staff and called down to Skip.

"Close, but I said to the end of the table!"

The rest of the IDP began to boo and otherwise voice their disapproval of Gar.

"Quiet!" shouted Colonel Lotar.

Skip rubbed the back of his neck and slowly rose to his feet as Colonel Lotar continued.

"Skip, I guess you'll remember to heed the exact meaning of any future orders; having said that, your performance here today has earned you the right to be heard."

The crowd echoed their approval.

Skip stood proudly, "Lieutenant Groon said that the laser turrets have motion sensors, right?" expecting an affirmative answer, Skip continued, "and I am assuming that when they find a moving object, they lock in on it and fire until the object is no longer moving, correct?"

"What are you getting at?" asked Lieutenant Groon.

Skip jumped back on the table. He was holding the middle of his jump rope and swinging the ends around alternating from side to side, faster and faster.

"If we cover my rope with Dr. Bosk's formula," Skip was now speaking louder over the whirring of the rope as it cut through the air. "You can use me as a decoy to draw the fire from the laser turrets while the rest of the team cross the ledge and destroy the factory."

Skip was spinning the rope very fast now, it was whistling through the air. Everyone was beginning to see how it might work.

Lieutenant Groon was standing next to Colonel Lotar and whispered in her ear. "You realize that he will have to keep that pace up for at least five minutes. If he stops or slows down, we are all sitting ducks."
Colonel Lotar whispered back, "Does it seem to you that he's getting tired, Lieutenant?"

Still spinning the rope, Skip moved closer to the head of the table where Colonel Lotar and Lieutenant Groon were standing.

"I think it's our best chance. What do you say Colonel?" asked Skip.

"I say that if I let you do this, and the plan works, you'll earn your IDP badge and we'll have a formal initiation ceremony." The Colonel hesitated a moment and then continued, "and if it doesn't work, we'll have a funeral for the entire commando unit."

The rest of the IDP listened intently for the final word.

"So either way, it looks like I need to clean my dress attire," she said.

CHAPTER

16

For the next few days, Skip, Joe, Dr. Bosk, Gar, Lieutenant Groon, Colonel Lotar, and Commander Aclovar discussed the plan to blow up the main Keebarian drug factory. The first order of business was to thoroughly test Lixablak.

Dr. Bosk took Skip's jump rope and began covering it with the glowing orange solution. Once it was·entirely covered, an energy field was formed and the rope began to glow even brighter.

Next, they tested the rope by firing many different weapons at it. It repelled them all.

Then, the real test. Skip picked up the rope and twirled the ends around as he had before. Nothing could penetrate the spinning force field.

Finally, the day came for them to put their plan into action. It was decided that a space pod would be the easiest vessel to slip past the Keebarian radar system because of its smaller size. Colonel Lotar chose Skip, Joe, Gar, Lieutenant Groon, and

Commander Aclovar as the commando unit for the mission.

As the IDP ship neared Keebar, they made final preparations in the conference room. They used the conference table as the narrow ledge, and four troopers, one in each corner, fired stun guns at Skip to act as laser turrets.

"Remember," said Lieutenant Groon, "we'll have a maximum of fifteen minutes to complete the mission. If you don't get back across the ledge in time, we'll have to assume you didn't make it."

The trial-runs improved with practice until they could estimate mission time of about twelve minutes. Filled with confidence, the group piled into the space pod and departed for Keebar.

The plan was to land in the wooded area west of the drug factory at nightfall. This would take exact timing, since Keebar has two suns and night comes only twice a week this time of year.

As the pod hovered and they waited to

land, everyone synchronized their timing devices. The explosives were set for 15 minutes and the timers would be activated when they left the ship. Skip's glowing rope was hidden in a knapsack so that no one would be spotted until they reached the ledge. They stared at each other as the pod touched down. The door opened. IT WAS SHOWTIME!

CHAPTER
fury on the Ledge

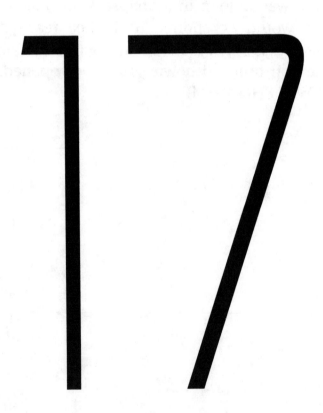

They made their way through a forest of barren trees, arriving near the ledge. The commando unit took shelter behind a bunker-like rock formation.

"Okay, kid," said Lieutenant Groon, "you're up."

Skip took out the rope and headed to the ledge. He began spinning the ends of the rope around him faster and faster. The glowing orange rope had a strobing effect against the black Keebarian sky as he stepped on to the ledge. The two closest laser turrets turned and started firing in Skip's direction.

"Here goes," thought Skip as he took a deep breath, "this time is for real."

The turrets locked in on the rope's movement and began firing at a semi-automatic pace. As Skip moved farther down the ledge the third turret swung around and locked-in. Dr. Bosk's Lixablak was working to perfection.

"One to go!" said Skip, (this time aloud).

But something was wrong. The 4th turret's motion sensor was facing the wrong way and hadn't noticed Skip's movement.

The others stood behind the rock bunker. They could all see that the 4th turret was not cooperating. Gar and Commander Aclovar began creeping out from behind the rocks.

"The plan was to wait for all four turrets to lock-in on Skip," Joe insisted.

"We can't wait forever!" blurted Gar.

"What is your assessment, Commander?" asked Lieutenant Groon.

"The turret could be jammed... it's hard to say from here," replied the Commander.

"We're still ahead of schedule," said Lieutenant Groon, after glancing at his timing device. "Let's give it just a little longer."

Gar was becoming more anxious with every passing second. He glared back at the Lieutenant, trying to get him to give the order.

Lieutenant Groon checked one more

time then said, forcefully, "Let's move out on my mark in 5...4...3...2...1."

Out of the corner of his eye, Skip saw the rest of them creeping toward the ledge. Suddenly, the forth turret began turning in their direction.

"Freeze!!" yelled Commander Aclovar. "Don't even blink."

Skip knew that if he didn't do something immediately, his defenseless comrades would all be gunned down.

While continuing to spin the rope, Skip ran down the ledge, trying to get the 4th turret's attention.

"No, not them! Over here!" he shouted.

Skip tried everything to attract the motion sensor. He jumped, turned, leaped, yelled, moonwalked, until finally the 4th turret turned and locked in, firing.

"Let's go!" said Lieutenant Groon as he sprinted onto the ledge.

The others followed, running so fast they nearly crashed into Skip before they all halted. The glow from the rope and the lasers cast a light on their faces. Suddenly, it occurred to each of them that they were about to pass through the eye of a hurricane of light, protected only by a jump rope and a Junior IDP agent!

Skip widened his legs and the four crawled through. He watched as they raced around the building. A shrill siren wailed into the night. Skip heard yelling and laser fire, but couldn't see very much. And then, from out of the darkness came a familiar voice that shook him to the very core of his being.

"Ichno Bleza Voskwa!"

"VARCO!" Skip yelled at the top of his lungs. But there was no response.

He could feel his heart pounding as he called out again, "VARCO!"

This time, Skip felt that his own voice sounded different...deeper. His vision began blurring and continued until he was completely blind.

"What's happening to me?" cried Skip, frightened.

He was trying desperately to maintain his balance on the ledge while still spinning the rope. He could only rely on his other senses to continue to deflect the laser fire.

But he was transforming. Bones

expanded. Muscles stretched. Every cell in his body was beginning to change.

And then, just as suddenly and mysteriously as the transformation began... it ended. His vision, appearance; everything returned to normal.

There was no time for him to consider what had just happened. Joe and Commander Aclovar came running out from the side of the building and back down the ledge. They crawled through Skip's outstretched legs and headed back to the space pod. There was no sign of Lieutenant Groon or Gar.

Precious seconds ticked away.

"C'mon...C'mon...where are they?" Skip was trying to remain calm as he glanced at his timing device which now read 4:03...4:02...4:01. Over the sounds of the siren, Skip heard a space ship being launched.

At last, Lieutenant Groon appeared from the far side of the building. He backed around the corner, firing his weapon at some pursuer that Skip could not see. He fired one last shot and then turned, running to the ledge.

As he reached Skip, he yelled out, "Everybody make it?"

"No, Gar's still out there," said Skip.

"There's only 3:24 left. We can't wait for him!"

And with that Lieutenant Groon crawled through Skip's legs and made his way to the end of the ledge. He turned around, expecting to find Skip right behind him, but he was still in the middle of the ledge waiting for Gar.

Before Lieutenant Groon could yell to Skip, Gar appeared from the building. He was holding one arm and limping as he struggled to get to the ledge.

Just as he stepped onto the ledge, Gar lost his footing, slipped and fell. Lieutenant Groon could only look on as Skip raced over to Gar.

In a matter of seconds, Skip had turned his body 180 degrees. As he backed toward Gar the turrets now fired at angles in front of him.

He spun both ends of the rope with one hand and with his spare hand reached down and pulled Gar back on to the ledge.

"Get on my back," Skip yelled to Gar.

Gar climbed on and while still spinning the rope, Skip ran all the way until they were both safely out of the turrets range, behind the bunker.

Lieutenant Groon helped Skip get Gar back through the woods and into the space pod.

"Let's get out of here!" said Joe, as he launched the ship.

The commando unit watched out of the small window as the Keebarian drug factory exploded into flames.

Skip applied first aid to Gar's arm and elevated his injured leg.

Gar turned to Skip and with a look of deep gratitude, said, "Whatever forces may be driving you...I'm just glad you're on our team." And with that, he offered Skip his hand in friendship.

CHAPTER

A Hero's Welcome

18

When the commando unit returned to the IDP ship, they were greeted with a hero's welcome.

Gar was rushed to the infirmary so that Dr. Bosk could examine and treat him.

Joe and Skip went back to their quarters to prepare their reports for the upcoming meeting, and to get some much needed rest. (It has been 37 Earth hours since they had slept.)

The next morning, on their way to the conference room, Joe and Skip stopped to look in on Gar. He was doing much better, and was happy to see some visitors.

The meeting was already buzzing with excitement when Skip and Joe arrived. Once again, they were greeted with thunderous applause, indicating approval from the IDP members. Colonel Lotar appeared, and everyone took their seats.

With a look of pride in her eyes, Colonel Lotar directed her attention to Skip and Joe.

"Congratulations to our commando

unit on a near flawless mission! And as promised, Skip will receive his official IDP badge tomorrow evening at the formal ceremonies."

There was another cheer from the crowd. Lieutenant Groon stood and addressed the meeting. "Initial reports showed that the Keebarian drug factory was completely destroyed, and that Varco was reported to be inside just before the bombing."

With this news, the crowd went wild. Lieutenant Groon, however, held up his hands to curtail their celebration.

He continued, "There was a single space ship that escaped before the explosion and Skip believes that Varco was on board that vessel."

Silence filled the room.

"We are closely monitoring several sectors to see if we can pick up the trail again, but as you know, once the Keebarians are close enough to transport themselves to a planet, searching for them is futile."

"Why is that?" asked Skip.

"Because Keebarians are space chameleons." replied Lieutenant Groon. "And that means that they have the ability to change their shape and blend in with any life form they choose."

"This was the best chance we've ever had of capturing Varco and he may have slipped through our fingers!" interjected Gar as he hobbled into the room. "I call for sanctions against those responsible!"

The stately Colonel Lotar quickly eased the mounting tension, "Well Gar, it's good to see that you are feeling better and are back to your old self. However, we can not dwell on the negatives. We have much to celebrate. Let us adjourn to prepare for tomorrow's ceremonies."

CHAPTER
The Chase is On

19

The formal ceremonies were magnificent. Each IDP member was dressed in his or her best outfit. There were lavish decorations, awards and fanfare.

Suddenly, Captain Clovis, the communications expert, burst into the hall. "We've picked up a lone Keebarian ship in sector two!" he exclaimed. "Looks like it's headed for Earth!"

"What is its estimated time of arrival?" asked Lieutenant Groon.

"Tomorrow at 14:16 hours - there is a chance we can intercept it, but we'll have to hurry," said Captain Clovis, as he turned to Colonel Lotar for the order.

It didn't take the Colonel long to decide.

"Set a course for Earth," she said, "when we get to sector 3, open the ship up - full thrusters."

The celebration ceremonies were postponed and everyone went back to their sleeping quarters to monitor the chase on their computer systems. The IDP ship would need to catch the Keebarians before they got within transport range of Earth. It was going to be very close, but still hours away. Skip sat down on his bed while Joe watched the screen for awhile.

"Joe, what were my parents like when you knew them?" asked Skip.

Joe thought for a moment, then said, "Where do I begin? It took an hour to deliver the eulogies at the memorial service. We were all best friends. There was something special about your parents. They loved themselves, each other and everyone that touched their lives. There was never a wasted moment with them. They took nothing for granted."

"And what about their decision to volunteer for the space program on Mars?" asked Skip. "How did they decide to leave everything and everybody they had known and loved?"

Joe paused. He chose his words very carefully. "Once your folks made a commitment, they never looked back. Ultimately, they went into space and gave their lives for the benefit of all mankind, including their family and friends."

CHAPTER
The Keebarians Surrender?

20

"Must have dozed off for a while," thought Skip, as he opened his eyes and stretched.

He glanced up at Joe who had fallen asleep while sitting at the computer.

"C'mon Joe, wake up! Its morning already!"

Skip nudged Joe's leg, but he continued to sleep. He lofted a pillow which hit Joe's shoulder and fell to the ground.

"Joe, what's the..."

To Skip's horror, Joe slumped in the chair and then slid lifelessly to the ground. As Skip reached his hand out for Joe, someone grabbed his arm from under the bed. It was Varco! Skip screamed and tried to pull his arm away from Varco's grip...then he heard Joe's voice...

"Skip...Skip! Wake up! You're having another nightmare!" Joe was tugging at Skip's arm.

Skip opened his eyes and sat up.

"I'm okay," he said. "Thanks for waking me."

Joe was about to update Skip on the status of the chase, when the computer beat him to it.

"The Keebarian ship will be in range of the tractor beam in 15 seconds...10, 9, 8..."

As they watched the monitor, Colonel Lotar made an announcement.

"The Keebarian ship has shut off its engines and lowered its defense shields. Looks like a surrender. Perhaps they are unaware that they are within transport range of Earth."

Skip followed Joe to the communications room, where Colonel Lotar, Lieutenant Groon and Captain Clovis were attempting to contact the Keebarian ship.

"No response, Colonel," said Captain Clovis. "I'm going to scan the ship for life forms."

Everyone waited anxiously for the scan results.

"Nothing," reported Clovis. "They must have already transported to Earth."

"The Keebarians are tricky," said

Colonel Lotar, "I want a search party sent aboard with micro-scanners to make sure they are not hiding or have transformed to a miniaturized state."

Four troopers volunteered to go aboard the Keebarian ship. Once on board, they split up and began micro-scanning each floor. Hours later, they returned to the IDP Ship, empty-handed.

CHAPTER

Skip Makes a Bold Request

21

Skip and Joe went to speak with Colonel Lotar, on the bridge.

"Send me to Earth, Colonel. I'll find Varco." Skip was very deliberate with his request.

"I'll go with him," said Joe.

Colonel Lotar looked at both men with concern.

"No Joe, we need you here. Besides, now that Varco has transformed himself, it might be impossible to find him."

"I've studied video tape of Varco every day for the past 15 years," said Skip. "I see him in my sleep...when I am able to sleep. No matter what he looks like on the outside, I know his every move and mannerism."

"Besides, once I figure out what this stuff is they're smuggling from Earth..." he held up the bag of paste-like substance, "...and where it comes from, I'll bet that Varco and the rest of the Keebarians will not be far away."

Colonel Lotar was reluctant, but after some thought decided to give Skip a chance.

"Remember, when you get to Earth, don't call attention to yourself. The Keebarians are all over the planet. Undoubtedly, they are in some very high positions. They might be able to recognize you from your involvement with us."

"Oh thank you Colonel, I won't let you down!" exclaimed Skip.

CHAPTER

Skip Prepares for His
Mission to Earth

22

Everyone gathered in the transport area for Skip's send-off to Earth. Colonel Lotar handed Skip a small electronic gadget.

"Take this transporter unit," she said. "When you need to be picked up, return to the original coordinates and activate this button."

Gar was holding a large brown box which he dropped on the table.

"We took these possessions from the captured Keebarians. It might be a good idea to look through these items."

Skip searched the box. There was a revolver, a stack of Earth currency and an identification badge that read "GIRTH". He decided to leave the gun. But he put the tag and money in his knapsack, along with his glowing rope, the video tape of Varco and his new IDP badge.

Lieutenant Groon told the computer to materialize a hologram of the planet Earth and pointed to the United States.

"We're going to send you to the general area where most of the space ship activity has been spotted. Are you ready to go?" he asked.

Colonel Lotar grabbed Skip by the shoulders and stared into his eyes, "Stay focused and be careful!" she urged. "Don't let your hatred of Varco make you reckless. If any of the Keebarians figure out that you're an IDP agent, they won't hesitate to kill you."

Gar stepped over to Skip. He was still limping slightly, "Our best to you," he said, "the success of our mission depends on you."

Joe embraced Skip. No words were exchanged. None were needed.

Captain Clovis indicated they were ready to transport.

"Let's go," said Skip as he gave Clovis a signal. And with that, he was gone.

CHAPTER

"Curse you Varco!"

23

As Skip walked along an old dirt road, an oppressive sun beat down on him. His mind began to wander back to thoughts of his parents and Varco, the creature in his bloodstream and his strange transformation on the ledge.

He remembered talking to his parents about what life on Earth might be like. So far, it was dry and dusty. He walked along for what seemed like hours until he saw a billboard along the road. It was still too far away to read...

Back on the IDP ship, Colonel Lotar and Lieutenant Groon were on the bridge discussing the IDP's next move. Captain Clovis picked up a distress signal coming from the Keebarian ship that was still being held in their tractor beam.

"Help me," said the voice. A visual link-up was made.

Lieutenant Groon was puzzled, "That's Beke, one of Gar's troopers. I just saw him about an hour ago by the transport area. Why would he go back to the Keebarian ship?"

Beke seemed to be in a great amount of pain. "I never left their ship," he strained to say, "there's a Keebarian among you, pretending to be me!"

Lieutenant Groon ran to the back of the communications room to check on the Keebarian prisoners. They were gone. The transporter showed a record of three life forms being sent to Earth about 45 minutes after Skip.

Colonel Lotar was furious, "Curse you Varco!" she yelled into the communications monitor. "You may have won this battle, but the war's not over yet!"

CHAPTER
So Many Questions

24

Back on Earth, Skip now stood beneath the shade of the large billboard. The sign was old and had been slightly faded by overexposure to the sun. However, he was able to make out the words, "Welcome to Borderville, Gateway to Leisure City", and then below, "Relax and Enjoy...You're in Girth Country!"

He looked at the badge in his knapsack. "Girth" was written on it in the same printing as the billboard. There were so many questions still to be answered...

✓ What is "Girth" and how are the Keebarians involved?

✓ What was the strange paste-like substance being smuggled from Earth?

✓ Could Skip really find Varco on a planet with billions of people?

These questions, and more will be answered in the next...

ADVENTURE OF THE
ROPE WARRIOR!

THE EARTH'S ENTIRE EXISTENCE
HANGS IN THE BALANCE
WHEN SKIP ROPER
RETURNS IN...

ADVENTURES
OF THE
ROPE WARRIOR™

SURVIVAL OF THE FIT

Leisure City has everything! *Moving sidewalks, voice-activated electronics, and a deliciously sinful pastry treat known as a "puff-puff".*

A couch potatoes paradise? or is this all part of the Keebarians evil plans?

NAME:	VARCO
HEIGHT:	6'0"
WEIGHT:	460 LBS.
HATCHED:	OCTOBER 26TH, 2042 (STANDARD EARTH TIME)
HOME:	KEEBAR

VARCO CAME INTO POWER IN 2068 WHEN HIS MILITANT GROUP OVERTHREW REIGNING KING WEESK. A GREAT WAR BROKE OUT AND MANY KEEBARIANS LOST THEIR LIVES.

VARCO EMERGED AS THE NEW RULER OF KEEBAR AND USED THE KEEBARIAN MILITARY TO BOLSTER HIS PROFITABLE DRUG OPERATION.

ALL KEEBARIANS ARE SPACE CHAMELEONS ABLE TO CHANGE THEIR SHAPE AND BLEND IN WITH ANY LIFEFORM.

SOME KEEBARIANS STILL OPPOSE VARCO AND WHAT HE STANDS FOR, BUT THEY ARE SMALL IN NUMBERS AND STAY IN HIDING.

NAME:	**DR. BOSK**
HEIGHT:	**5'3"**
WEIGHT:	**680 LBS.**
BIRTHDAY:	**MAY 7TH, 2003**
	(STANDARD EARTH TIME)
HOME:	**KROM**

DR. BOSK HEADS THE MEDICAL STAFF FOR THE INTERGALACTICAL DRUG POLICE. HE LEFT HIS JOB AS CHIEF SURGEON AT RIVER VALLEY GENERAL (ROUGHLY TRANSLATED) TO JOIN THE IDP IN 2061.

DR. BOSK ATTENDED MEDICAL SCHOOL AT TURIEK UNIVERSITY WHERE HE MAJORED IN INTERPLANETARY ANATOMY. HIS POST GRADUATE STUDIES HAVE BEEN DEVOTED TO EXPERIMENTATION WITH A RARE SUB-STANCE KNOWN AS MISSONIUM.

DR. BOSK LOVES TO TELL A GOOD JOKE; MAYBE SOMEDAY HE'LL LEARN ONE.

NAME:	COLONEL LOTAR
HEIGHT:	5' 10"
WEIGHT:	130 LBS.
BIRTHDAY:	JULY 17TH, 2014 (STANDARD EARTH TIME)
HOME:	RUXA

FROM THE MOMENT SHE WAS BORN LIMA LOTAR WAS DESTINED FOR GREATNESS. HER FATHER WAS A HIGHLY DECORATED GENERAL AND HER MOTHER WAS A WEALTHY SOCIALITE.

WITH HER GRACE, CHARISMA, AND STRONG LEADERSHIP QUALITIES, COLONEL LOTAR WAS THE UNANIMOUS CHOICE OF THE COUNCIL TO COMMAND THE IDP SHIP.

COLONEL LOTAR HAS A FONDNESS FOR WA-AM-BUL MILK WHICH SHE DRINKS WITH A SPLASH OF FWEETSY JUICE.

NAME:	**LT. GROON**
HEIGHT:	**6'1"**
WEIGHT:	**870 LBS.**
BIRTHDAY:	**FEBRUARY 15TH, 2045 (STANDARD EARTH TIME)**
HOME:	**RL7 SECTOR**

LT. GROON JOINED THE IDP IN 2066 AFTER DR. BOSK SAVED HIS LIFE DURING THE "GREAT SECTORIAN WAR".

LT. GROON HAD LED AN ATTACK SQUADRON OVER ENEMY LINES INTO SECTOR 6. HIS SHIP WAS SHOT DOWN AND GROON WAS LEFT FOR DEAD.

DR. BOSK HAD BEEN VISITING A MEDICAL UNIT IN THE FIELD NEAR THE FRONT LINE WHEN HE GOT WORD OF THE WAR HERO'S DEMISE. PLAYING A HUNCH, DR. BOSK TRANSPORTED HIMSELF BACK TO THE IDP SHIP AND SEARCHED FOR LT. GROON. WHEN THEY FOUND HIM, THE SHIP WAS IN BAD SHAPE, AND GROON WAS IN WORSE. USING PIECES FROM THE FALLEN SHIP, DR. BOSK WELDED TOGETHER A NEW AND IMPROVED LT. GROON.

JOIN THE OFFICIAL
ROPE WARRIOR FAN CLUB!

First Year ***Membership Includes:***

-AN AUTOGRAPHED, LIMITED
 EDITION ROPE WARRIOR TRADING CARD.

-FOUR FULL COLOR POSTERS (11"x17")

-A ROPENASTICS™ INSTRUCTION
 BOOKLET (INCLUDES 25 TRICKS)

-A GLOW IN THE DARK
 ROPE WARRIOR BUTTON

-A QUARTERLY NEWSLETTER

ONLY
$14.95

OFFER EXPIRES 4/25/98
MEMBERSHIP GOOD FOR ONE YEAR FROM DATE OF RECEIPT

ABOUT THE AUTHOR

David L Fisher *AKA The Rope Warrior* is an accomplished businessman and entertainer. His dedication to the health and well-being of people everywhere resulted in his developing an innovative Dance/Sport/Fitness program called ROPENASTICS™. ROPENASTICS™ is a combination of rope jumping, dance, aerobics, and rhythmic gymnastics.

David's list of performances and
television appearances include:

The NBC Nightly News
with Tom Brokaw

Toku Ho Okoku (Nippon
Television Network)

The Today Show

The Inner City Games

NBA and NFL Halftime
Shows

Real Life

Opening Ceremonies of
the Goodwill Games in
St. Petersburg, Russia

The Jenny Jones Show

Energy Express

Brachita

For information on public appearances, workshops,
or new products Call Toll Free at:
1-888-JMP-ROPE
Remember the only thing missing is "U"

http://www.ropewarrior.com